Adapted by Victoria Saxon

Based on the screenplay by
Kacey Arnold and Kate Boutilier

Illustrated by
Charles Pickens and Patrick Ian Moss

First published in Great Britain 2016 by Egmont UK Limited
The Yellow Building, 1 Nicholas Road, London W11 4AN

ISBN 978 1 4052 8435 6
64048/1
Printed in Italy

Once upon a time, on the far-away planet of Para-Den, lived a very special girl named Barbie. Barbie lived with her father, and together they took care of all the planet's different animals.

Barbie was very talented at hoverboarding, and she liked to swoop around the planet and fly with the Ava-Grun birds. She loved all the animals on Para-Den.

Barbie had another special talent. When she focussed and listened to the music around her, Barbie could move objects with her mind! As Barbie practised, her skills got better and better. Today, she was able to focus and build a nest for a family of birds!

Barbie's pet, Pupcorn, flew along beside her. Someday Pupcorn would "pop" and transform into a different animal like a dog, a cat or even a zebra! But Barbie didn't know yet which animal he would become.

Later that afternoon, a droid landed outside Barbie's house with a message for her father.

"The king has heard of your hoverboarding skills, and he has chosen you to help with his mission to save the stars from disappearing!" Barbie's father announced.

"Why would the stars disappear?" Barbie asked sadly. She couldn't imagine a world without stars!

"Your mother used to say it was because people stopped looking up. The stars had no one to dance with anymore."

That night, Barbie's father found her outside.

"I'm not sure I can do this," Barbie admitted. "I've never left Para-Den before."

Barbie's father smiled gently. "Remember what your mother always used to say: 'Search your heart for the answer, and follow it to the end'."

Barbie touched the locket her mother had given her long again. She knew exactly what she needed to do.

Barbie's father flew with her to Oppa-Irri, King Constantine's home planet. Before he left, he gave her two gifts – a ballgown from her mother and a brand-new hoverboard!

"Good luck, my little Starlight," he said, giving Barbie a big hug.

That evening, Barbie met the other recruits. They had been chosen from all over the galaxy for their special skills. Sal-Lee was the intergalactic hoverboarding champion. Twins Kareena and Sheena had a talent for manipulating gravity – and changing colours. And Prince Leo was the fastest pilot in the galaxy.

Everyone was so friendly that Barbie felt at home at once. Kareena and Sheena sat down next to Barbie. Then they both changed colour!

"I'm Sheena –"

"– and I'm Kareena! We're thrilled –"

"– to meet you," they said at once.

Later the recruits started dancing. Barbie used the
sounds around her to create a new song. Soon everyone
was having a ball!

Unfortunately, King Constantine was not pleased.
"This is not how we do things," he warned Barbie.
"I have my eye on you."

The next morning, King Constantine and his robotic assistant, Artemis, explained the mission to the recruits.

"According to the prophecy, if we do not get the stars to dance again, they will disappear," Artemis said.

The king presented a machine called the Stato-Tron.

"This machine will shock the stars back into dancing," the king explained. His plan was to get the machine to the heart of the galaxy and reset the stars with an electric jolt.

Barbie frowned. It didn't sound right to shock the stars back into dancing.

It was time for their training to begin. Barbie and Sal-Lee were racing while Sheena and Kareena moved obstacles out of the way with their powers. As the race was about to end, Barbie used her mind to move two blocks that were going to squash Sal-Lee!

Constantine was intrigued by Barbie's ability to move matter.

"I was unaware of this power you have, Barbie," Constantine said. He made Barbie practise splitting large cubes in the training area.

Barbie focussed as hard as she could, but she was already tired. Soon, the block was too much for her.

After the training session, Sal-Lee spoke
to Barbie.

"The king was a little tough on you,"
Sal-Lee said.

Barbie smiled as Sal-Lee took off on her
hoverboard. It was nice to have friends!

Barbie gave Pupcorn a hug, and then she
noticed something strange. Pupcorn had
grown whiskers!

Pupcorn had popped!

The little space creature had transformed into an adorable cat. Pupcorn could no longer fly, so Barbie spent the night creating a special spacesuit just for him.

The next day, the king sent the team on one more training exercise.

"You'll be capturing a Starlian and bringing it back to me," he told them, but he was looking mostly at Barbie. He was still unsure about her.

Barbie was determined to do a good job. She took the lead as the team headed out on the test.

They soon landed successfully on the planet and began
searching for the Starlian.

"Did you hear that?" Barbie cried as they explored the strange
planet. She took off, and the other recruits followed after her.

Suddenly, the mysterious Starlian came out from its
hiding place. Barbie began to drum, and the others
joined in. The Starlian was so mesmerised by the
music, Barbie could use special equipment to
capture him.

But Barbie could see the Starlian was
scared. Concerned for the kind-hearted
creature, Barbie freed him from
the net.

King Constantine was furious. "I needed a Starlian to guide us to the centre of the galaxy!" he roared. "They're the only creatures that can protect us from the magnetic storms."

"Why didn't you say that?" Barbie asked. But the king would not forgive Barbie. He eliminated her from the team.

Barbie called her father. "Dad," Barbie said, "I felt like I did the right thing, but I put my friends in danger!"

"Just tell me what happened. You might be able to fix it," her father replied calmly.

"That's it. I can fix it. And I'm the only one who can," Barbie said. "Gotta go, Dad, love you!"

Meanwhile, the rest of the team were disappointed.
"We're not much of a team now," said Leo.
The others agreed. How could they continue their
mission without Barbie?

Sal-Lee went to the king to ask him to bring Barbie back.
"Barbie knows how to be a leader," Sal-Lee said. "It takes heart."
Just then Barbie appeared with the Starlian! Reluctantly,
Constantine let Barbie back on the team.

The next morning, the king's ship sped towards the heart of the galaxy. "I must fulfil the prophecy," the king said. "The people must know I saved the galaxy."

They were all grateful when the Starlian guided them through the frightening and turbulent magnetic storms.

Suddenly, a chunk of debris crashed into one of the ship's thrusters!

Leo exited the ship and removed the rocks and other space rubbish. Then more debris knocked Leo, and he was floating away!

Barbie instructed the twins to pull Leo back to the ship with their gravity skills.

"You can do this," Barbie said encouragingly. "Trust me."

With Barbie at the lead, the plan worked! Leo was saved, and soon the ship was back on track.

They arrived at a deep cavern, where they found a bright star.
It was the heart of the galaxy.

King Constantine moved everyone else out of the way as he
set up the Stato-Tron.

The machine sent out a huge charge of electricity, causing
the cavern to shake. When it stopped, the king gasped.

"They aren't dancing!" he said as he looked at the stars.

Barbie watched as the stars seemed to fade and drop.
She caught one tiny, fading star in her hand.
She had to do something before all of the stars disappeared!

As more stars fell, Barbie heard something.

"It's a song," Barbie said. "Can you hear it?" She put her hand on her mother's locket, stepped deeper into the caverns and began to sing. After a moment, Barbie's friends joined her.

The stars flickered to life, glowing brightly. The stars were dancing!

Barbie was filled with joy. "We just needed to remember to look up and dance," she said.

As the friends sang and laughed, their combined energy created so much power that Barbie started to glow and hover. Then, with a flash, the stars shot out of the tunnel and into the skies, exploding like a shockwave across the galaxy. The stars danced back into their orbits and the entire galaxy was saved!

Back at King Constantine's palace, Barbie's father met her at the celebratory ball.

"I'm so proud of you, my little Starlight," he said. Then he chuckled, and added, "Excuse me – Princess Starlight."

King Constantine, admitting that he was wrong about Barbie, had given her a new title: Princess!

From now on, Princess Starlight would make sure that there would be plenty of songs – and lots of dancing – throughout the galaxy.

THE END